THE INCREDIBLE HULK™

Larger Than Life

By Lisa Rao
Based on the screenplay by Zak Penn and Edward Norton
Illustrated by YOE! Studio®

simon scribbles

New York   London   Toronto   Sydney

An imprint of Simon & Schuster Children's Publishing Division
1230 Avenue of the Americas, New York, NY 10020

Book manufactured in the United States of America
Grow-Your-Own-Hulk manufactured in China
First Edition
2 4 6 8 10 9 7 5 3 1
ISBN-13: 978-1-4169-6088-1
ISBN-10: 1-4169-6088-0

Bruce Banner is an American hiding out in Brazil. He works at a soda factory. He keeps to himself. Bruce has a secret. . . .

Bruce used to be a scientist. He worked with gamma radiation to see if it could make people stronger. Bruce tried it on himself.

But the gamma radiation did more than make him stronger.
It turned him into a completely different person, if you could call it
a person. When he gets angry, Bruce turns into . . .

THE INCREDIBLE HULK!

When Bruce turns into The Incredible Hulk, he can't control himself.
People get hurt. Bruce doesn't want that to happen.
He avoids getting angry. He monitors his pulse to make sure he's not
getting too excited. He meditates and practices yoga to stay calm.

Bruce searched the Internet trying to find someone who could help him.
He contacted a scientist with the code name Mr. Blue. Mr. Blue thinks
there is an antidote that will stop Bruce from turning into The Hulk!
Mr. Blue tells Bruce about a special liquid.
It comes from a rare flower that only grows in South America.

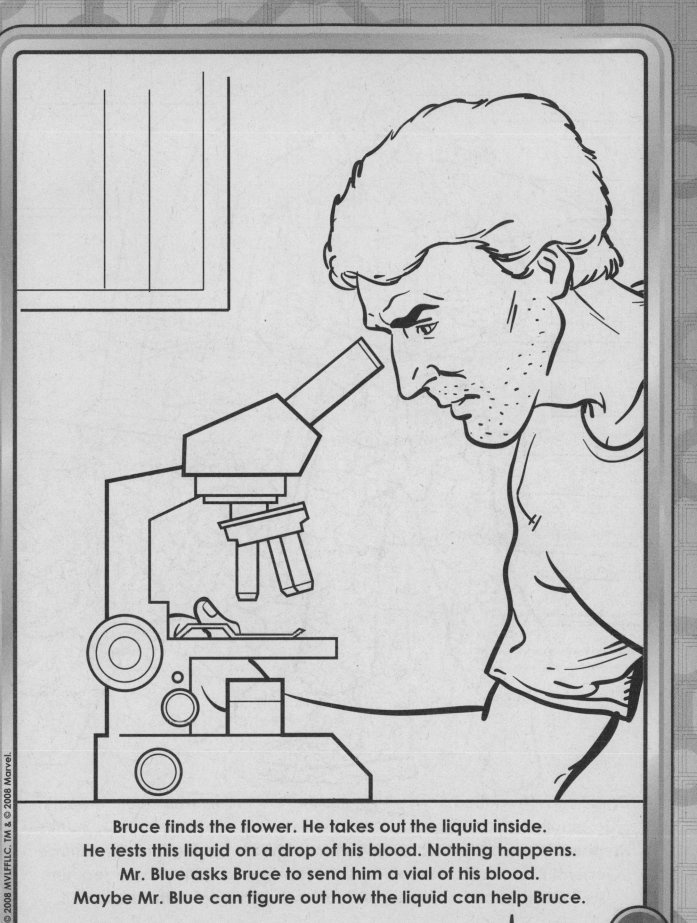

Bruce finds the flower. He takes out the liquid inside.
He tests this liquid on a drop of his blood. Nothing happens.
Mr. Blue asks Bruce to send him a vial of his blood.
Maybe Mr. Blue can figure out how the liquid can help Bruce.

Meanwhile the United States government has been searching for Bruce.
General Ross wants to know how the gamma radiation changed him.
He tracks Bruce down and flies to Brazil with a Special Forces unit.

Emil Blonsky is the leader of the Special Forces unit.
General Ross tells him about Bruce.

The Special Forces unit goes to Bruce's apartment to find him.
But Bruce leaves before they can catch him.

As Bruce runs away from the Special Forces unit, some tough guys notice him. They're looking for a fight. "Let me go," says Bruce. "You don't understand. Something really bad is going to happen here."

13

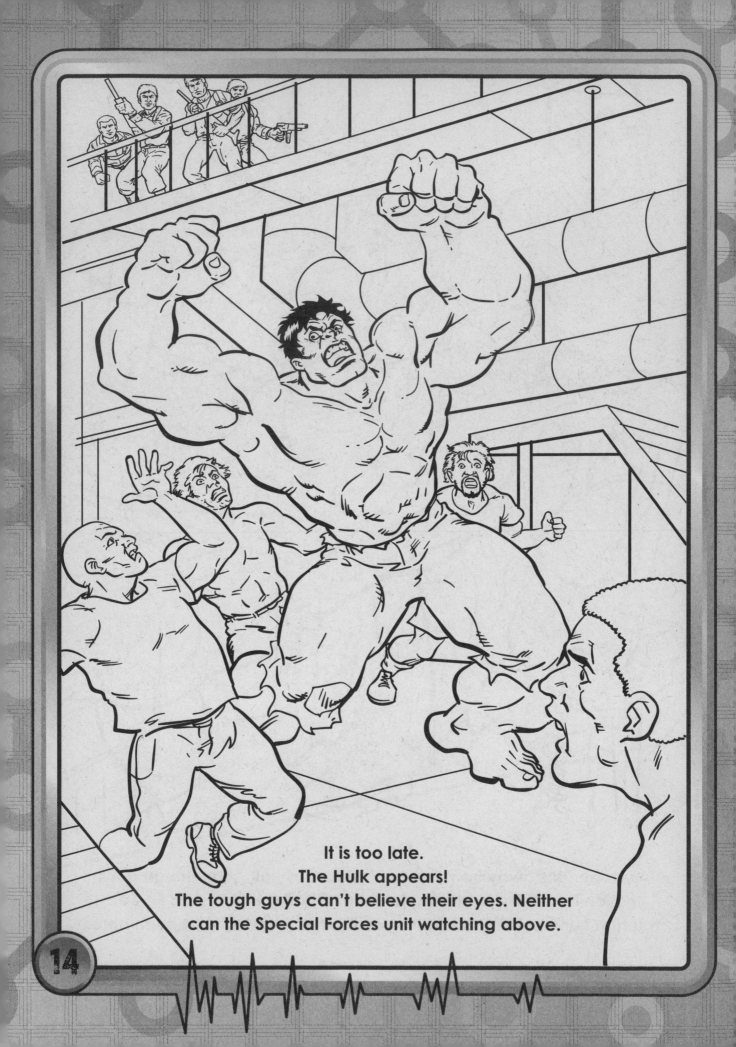

It is too late.
The Hulk appears!
The tough guys can't believe their eyes. Neither can the Special Forces unit watching above.

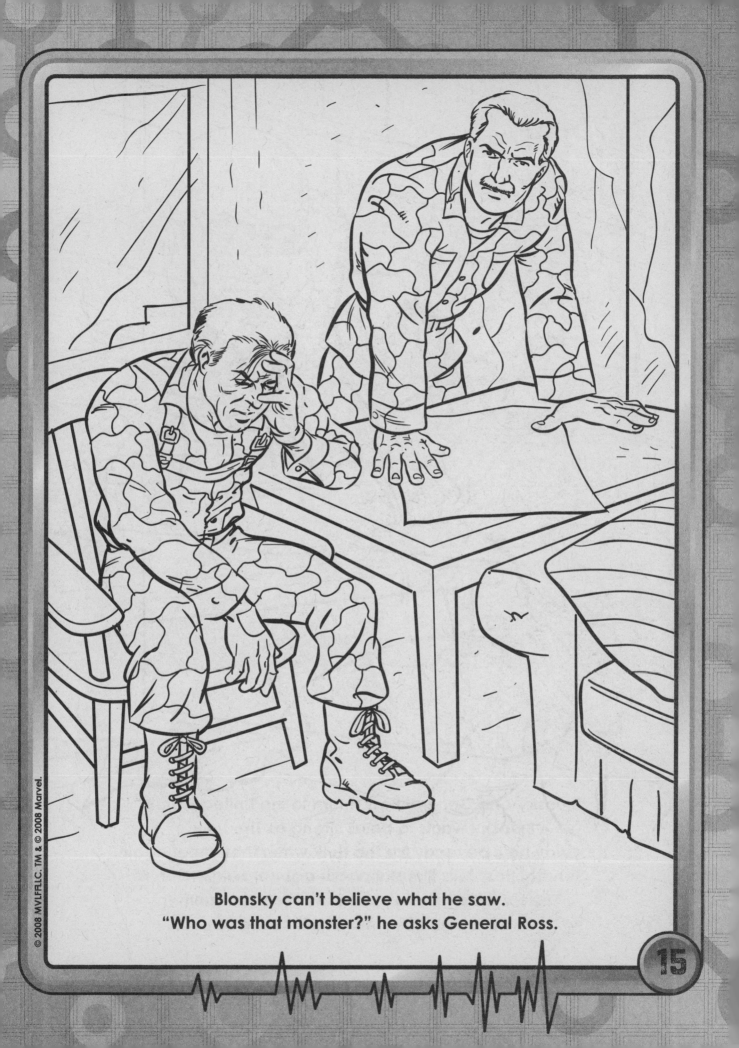

Blonsky can't believe what he saw.
"Who was that monster?" he asks General Ross.

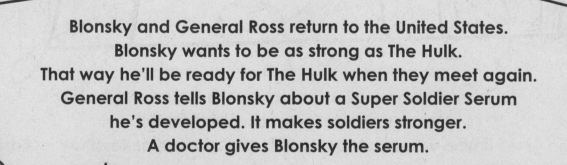

Blonsky and General Ross return to the United States.
Blonsky wants to be as strong as The Hulk.
That way he'll be ready for The Hulk when they meet again.
General Ross tells Blonsky about a Super Soldier Serum
he's developed. It makes soldiers stronger.
A doctor gives Blonsky the serum.

Bruce also returns to the United States.
Mr. Blue needs more information about his gamma radiation.
Bruce runs into Betty, his old girlfriend.
She gives Bruce a computer chip with the information Mr. Blue needs!

Betty's new boyfriend, Samson, makes a
private phone call to General Ross.
He tells him where Bruce is!

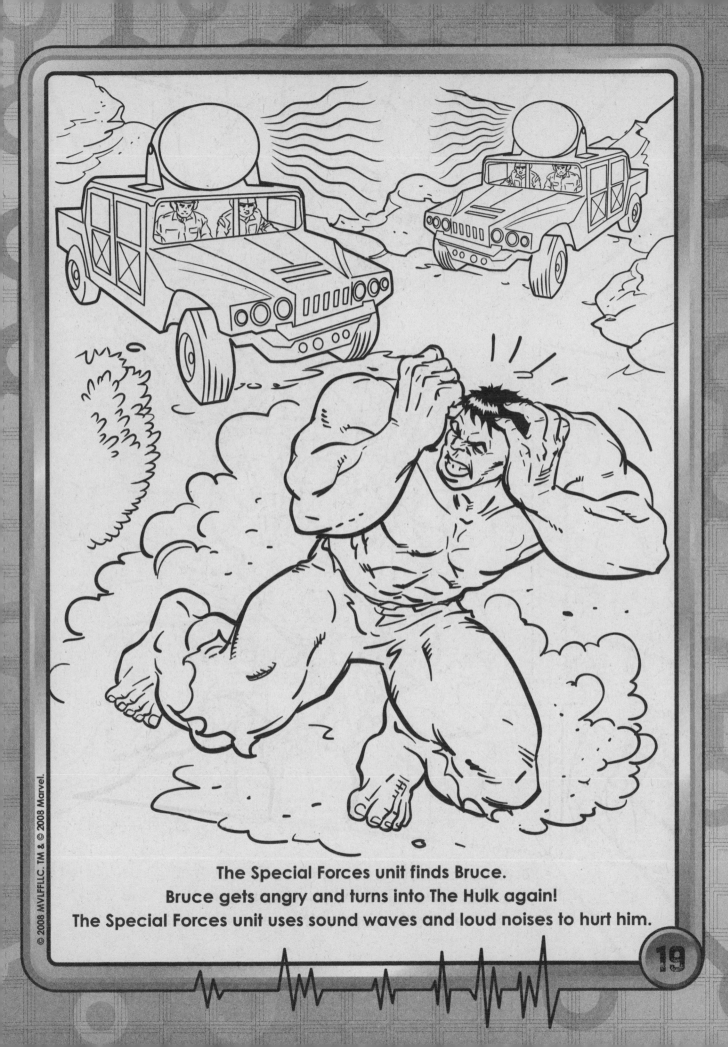

The Special Forces unit finds Bruce.
Bruce gets angry and turns into The Hulk again!
The Special Forces unit uses sound waves and loud noises to hurt him.

Blonsky tries to fight The Hulk but he is no match.
He is badly hurt and brought to the nearest hospital.

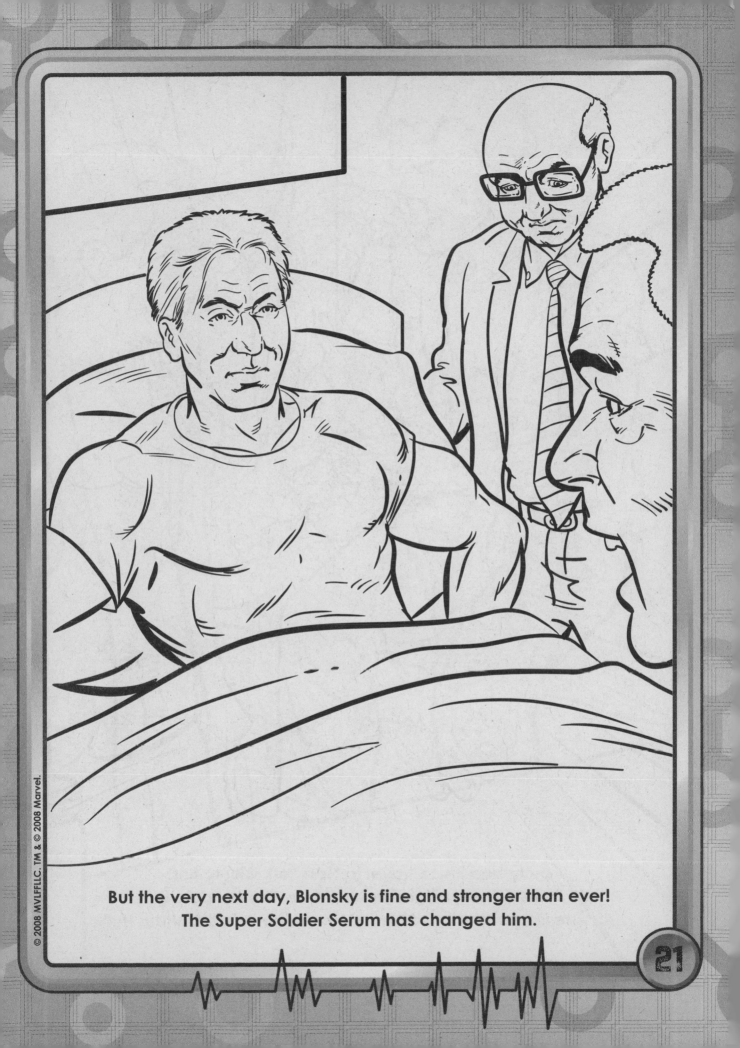

But the very next day, Blonsky is fine and stronger than ever!
The Super Soldier Serum has changed him.

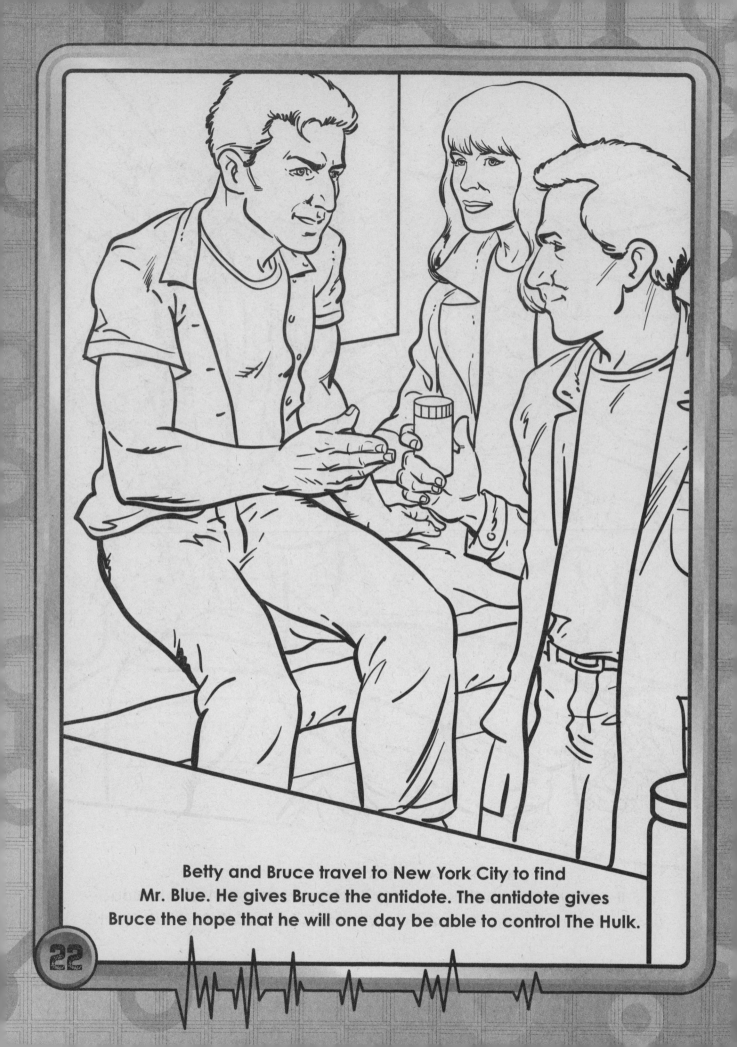

Betty and Bruce travel to New York City to find
Mr. Blue. He gives Bruce the antidote. The antidote gives
Bruce the hope that he will one day be able to control The Hulk.

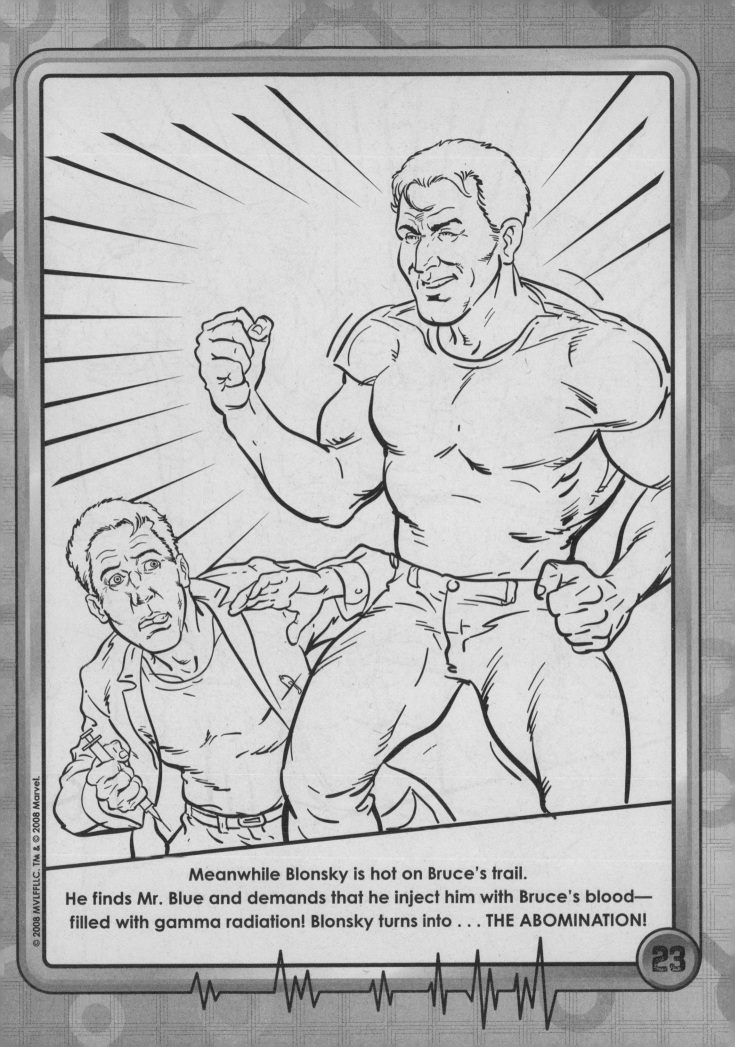

Meanwhile Blonsky is hot on Bruce's trail.
He finds Mr. Blue and demands that he inject him with Bruce's blood—
filled with gamma radiation! Blonsky turns into . . . THE ABOMINATION!

23

Now it's The Incredible Hulk versus The Abomination. . . .
Who will win?